# THE SHEEP OF SLEEP

words by Geoff Isenman     pictures by Michael Scott

D1361071

Their houses are made of hay.
And their grocery stores sell grass and clover.

Like the other lambs who live there,
Cal knew just what he wanted to be when he grew up.

Not an astronaut.

Or a fireman.

Not a doctor.

Or a beekeeper.

No, Cal dreamed about being one of the
Sheep of Sleep.
They are a special team who help boys and girls
all over the world get a good night's rest.

But Cal was still just a lamb.

One night Cal broke the rules.
The sleep alarm sounded, and
he secretly flew off to face one of
the scariest creatures in the world.

A cranky little person who does not want to go to bed.

The sheep team arrived,
and the girl counted:
One sheep, two sheep, three sheep, four.
Five sheep, six sheep, seven sheep, more...

Twelve sheep, thirteen, fourteen, **FIFTEEN!**
She was not ready to fall asleep.
Cal began to worry that sneaking out was a bad idea.

He tried to be brave though
and did something unexpected:
'Baaah,' Cal said to the girl.

And with one more Baah,
the girl's eyes finally closed.

The Sheep of Sleep were grateful for Cal's help,
but joining the team would have to wait.
Cal had to go face two very worried creatures.

A mother and father
who did not know where their little lamb was.

And Cal fell asleep...

...Meanwhile, the Sheep of Sleep practiced a new drill.